Frogs in the Bed

My Passover Seder Activity Book

By Ann D. Koffsky

Based on the song by Shirley Cohen Steinberg

BEHRMAN HOUSE

www.behrmanhouse.com

In memory of my cousin, Diane Susan Thurer,
who made all my childhood seders wonderful.
—AK

To all my children and to the many preschoolers
I have taught who were a source of inspiration to me.
—SCS

Editor: Dena Neusner
Design: David Neuhaus/NeuStudio

Activities and Illustrations copyright © 2014 by Ann D. Koffsky
"One Morning (The Frog Song)" copyright © 1951 by Shirley Cohen Steinberg

Published by Behrman House, Inc., Springfield, New Jersey 07081
ISBN 978-0-87441-913-9 • Printed in China

Visit www.behrmanhouse.com/passover

when Pharaoh awoke in bed,

there were frogs in the bed . . .

and frogs on his head,

frogs on his nose...

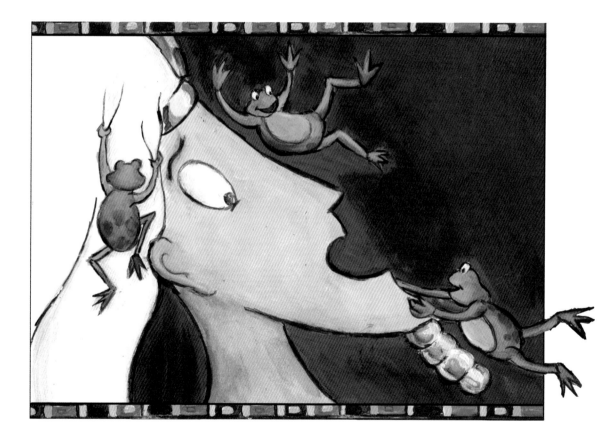

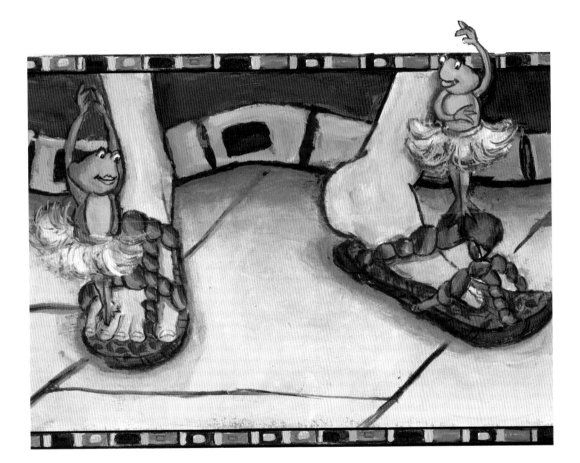

and frogs on his toes.

Frogs there!

Frogs just jumping everywhere!

Seder Symbol Strings

On the seder plate, we have a collection of unusual foods. Each of the foods is a symbol—an object that can teach us something about the holiday. Follow the strings and match each food on the seder plate to the idea it reminds us of.

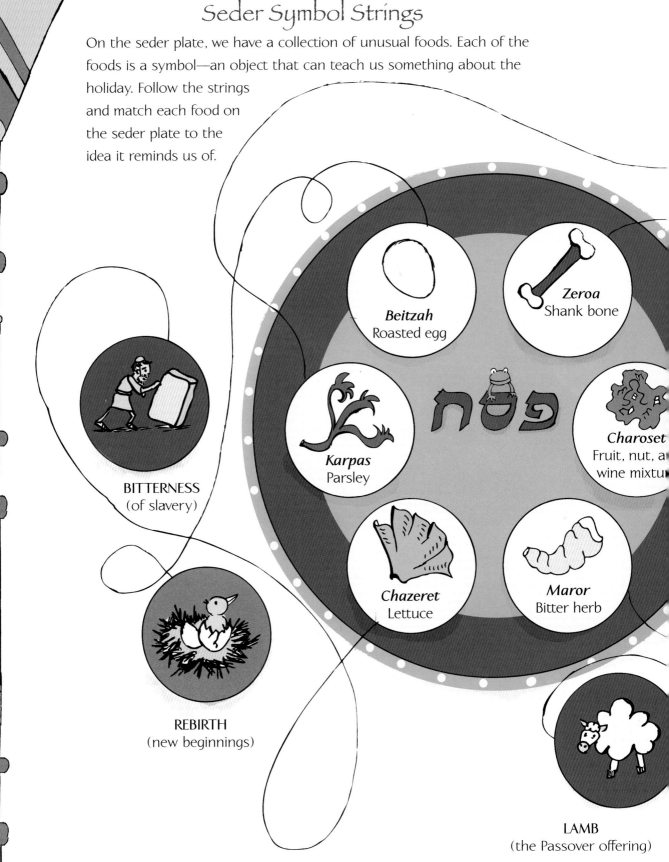

BITTERNESS
(of slavery)

REBIRTH
(new beginnings)

LAMB
(the Passover offering)

Beitzah
Roasted egg

Zeroa
Shank bone

Karpas
Parsley

Charoset
Fruit, nut, a[nd]
wine mixtu[re]

Chazeret
Lettuce

Maror
Bitter herb

SPRING
(new life and hope)

MORTAR
(glue used with bricks)

BITTERNESS
(of slavery)

קַדֵּשׁ

Four Cups

We will drink four cups of wine or grape juice at our seder. Can
you tell which of these four cups is different from all the others?

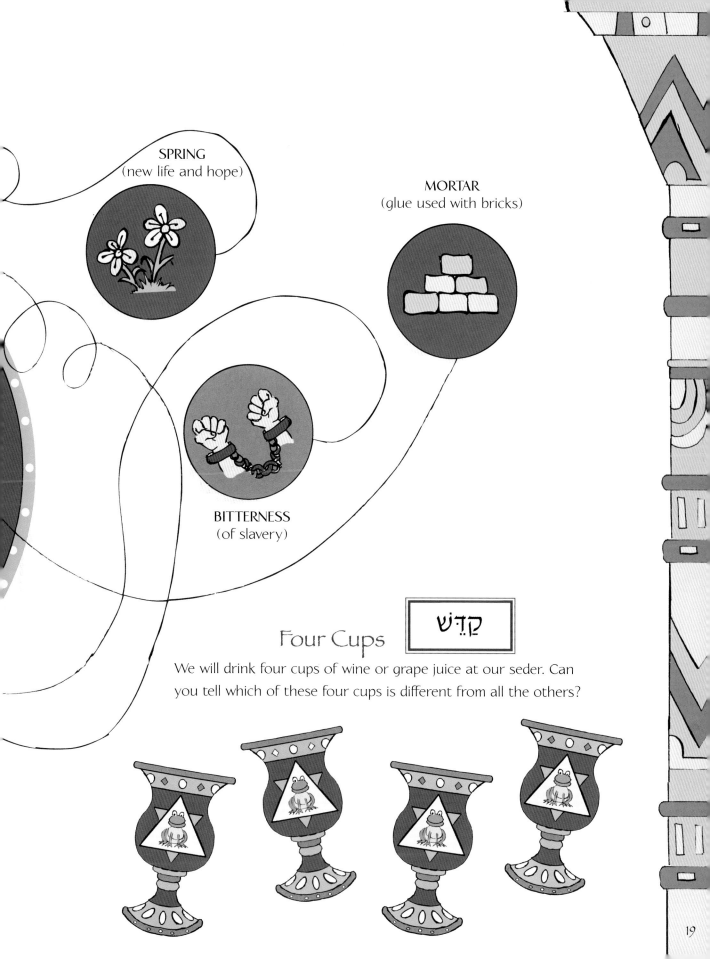

Mah Nishtanah: The Four Questions

מַה נִּשְׁתַּנָּה הַלַּיְלָה הַזֶּה מִכָּל הַלֵּילוֹת?

Mah nishtanah halailah hazeh mikol haleilot?

Why is this night different from all other nights?

שֶׁבְּכָל הַלֵּילוֹת אָנוּ אוֹכְלִין חָמֵץ וּמַצָּה.
הַלַּיְלָה הַזֶּה כֻּלּוֹ מַצָּה.

Sheb'chol haleilot anu och'lin chameitz umatzah.
Halailah hazeh kulo matzah.

On all other nights we eat either leavened or
unleavened bread, but on this night we eat only
matzah, unleavened bread.

שֶׁבְּכָל הַלֵּילוֹת אָנוּ אוֹכְלִין שְׁאָר יְרָקוֹת.
הַלַּיְלָה הַזֶּה מָרוֹר.

Sheb'chol haleilot anu och'lin sh'ar y'rakot.
Halailah hazeh maror.

On all other nights we eat all kinds of herbs,
but on this night we eat only bitter herbs.

שֶׁבְּכָל הַלֵּילוֹת אֵין אָנוּ מַטְבִּילִין אֲפִילוּ פַּעַם
אֶחָת. הַלַּיְלָה הַזֶּה שְׁתֵּי פְעָמִים.

Sheb'chol haleilot ein anu matbilin afilu pa'am echat.
Halailah hazeh sh'tei f'amim.

On all other nights we do not dip herbs even once,
but on this night we dip twice.

שֶׁבְּכָל הַלֵּילוֹת אָנוּ אוֹכְלִין בֵּין יוֹשְׁבִין וּבֵין מְסֻבִּין.
הַלַּיְלָה הַזֶּה כֻּלָּנוּ מְסֻבִּין.

Sheb'chol haleilot anu och'lin bein yoshvin uvein m'subin.
Halailah hazeh kulanu m'subin.

On all other nights we eat either sitting or reclining,
but on this night we all recline.

Magid and Miracles: A Passover Comic

It's time for *magid*, telling the story of Passover. Read it with a friend.

A LONG TIME AGO, OUR ANCESTORS LIVED IN EGYPT. THEY BUILT HOMES AND RAISED THEIR FAMILIES THERE.

YOU MUST ALL BE MY SLAVES!

THEN A NEW PHARAOH BECAME THE RULER, AND HE DID NOT LIKE THE ISRAELITES, AS OUR PEOPLE WERE CALLED.

GOD SENT MOSES TO SPEAK WITH PHARAOH.

PLEASE! YOU MUST LET MY PEOPLE GO!

NO WAY! YOU CAN'T GO.

TO CONVINCE PHARAOH TO CHANGE HIS MIND, GOD MADE MANY PLAGUES.

BLOOD FROGS LICE WILD BEASTS CATTLE DISEASE

DURING EACH PLAGUE, PHARAOH PROMISED MOSES HE WOULD LET THE ISRAELITES GO.

OKAY, OKAY, GO ALREADY! JUST STOP THIS HORRIBLE PLAGUE!

BUT AS SOON AS THE PLAGUE ENDED, PHARAOH CHANGED HIS MIND.

I WAS JUST KIDDING. YOU CAN'T GO!

BOILS HAIL LOCUSTS DARKNESS DEATH OF FIRSTBORN

FINALLY, AFTER THE TENTH PLAGUE, PHARAOH ALLOWED THE ISRAELITES TO LEAVE EGYPT. THEY RUSHED OUT SO FAST, THEY DIDN'T HAVE TIME FOR THEIR BREAD TO RISE. INSTEAD, THE SUN BAKED THE DOUGH AND IT BECAME MATZAH.

HURRY!

BUT PHARAOH CHANGED HIS MIND AGAIN. HE CHASED THE ISRAELITES UNTIL THEY WERE TRAPPED BETWEEN HIS SOLDIERS AND THE SEA OF REEDS. THE ISRAELITES WERE STUCK!

JUST WHEN THEY THOUGHT IT WAS ALL OVER, GOD SPLIT THE WATERS OF THE SEA! THE ISRAELITES WALKED SAFELY THROUGH TO THE OTHER SIDE.

PHARAOH'S ARMY TRIED TO CHASE THEM . . . BUT THE WAVES CRASHED DOWN ONTO THE SOLDIERS. OUR PEOPLE WERE NOW TRULY FREE.

Munchy Matzah

It's time to munch some matzah!

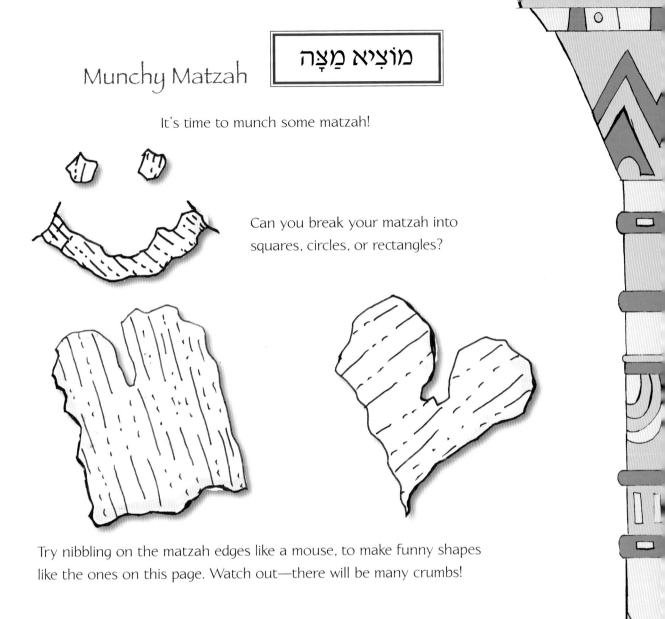

Can you break your matzah into squares, circles, or rectangles?

Try nibbling on the matzah edges like a mouse, to make funny shapes like the ones on this page. Watch out—there will be many crumbs!

You can use charoset to attach two matzah shapes together and make a new shape. Give your crazy matzah shape a name.

Maror: Faces, Feelings, and Freedom

מָרוֹר

We eat maror, the bitter herb, at the seder
to remember the bitterness of slavery.

Taste the maror. Go ahead, make a
face or draw one here to show
how you would feel if you
were a slave.

How would you feel when you are freed?

Silly Seder Scene

Is it time to eat already? This seder is not quite the way it should be!
Can you find at least ten weird, wacky, or silly things in the picture?

Find the Afikoman

Oh no! The afikoman is missing, and we can't finish the seder!
Complete the maze to find the afikoman.

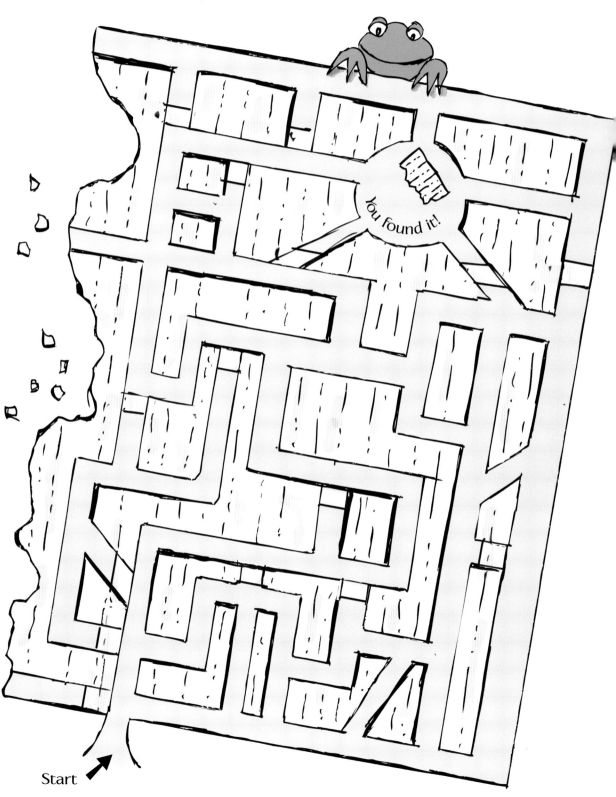

You found it!

Start

Sparkly Elijah's Cup

Place this sparkly glass proudly in the center of the seder table to welcome the prophet Elijah. If your seder includes a Miriam's Cup, design a glass with her name on it, too.

You will need:

- A sturdy plain or plastic wine glass
- Glitter
- Masking tape
- Mod Podge glue
- Small paintbrush

1

2

Directions:

1. Make sure your glass is clean and dry. Wrap a piece of masking tape around the center of your glass, as shown.

2. Use a paintbrush to apply Mod Podge to the glass below the tape line. Paint the name "ELIJAH" in Mod Podge above the tape line.

3. Sprinkle glitter so that it sticks to all the Mod Podge. Let it dry, and then remove the tape. Apply another coat of Mod Podge over the glitter to seal it in place.

Note: After the seder, hand wash carefully.

3

Welcoming Elijah

At the seder, we open the door to welcome Elijah.
Can you sing along to "Eliyahu Hanavi?"

Eliyahu hanavi, Eliyahu haTishbi,
Eliyahu, Eliyahu, Eliyahu haGiladi,
Bimheirah v'yameinu yavo eileinu,
im Mashiach ben David, im Mashiach ben David.

Jumping Froggie

Let this fun frog hop around your seder table as you sing
"One Morning (The Frog Song)."

You will need:

Markers or crayons
Paper
Scissors
Glue stick or clear tape
Googly eyes
2 rubber bands
1 sturdy paper cup
1 cardboard paper towel or toilet paper roll

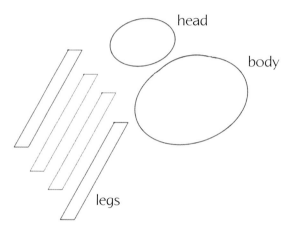

Directions:

1. Trace the shapes from the inside back cover.
   Color them and cut them out.

2. Fold each of the legs
   accordion-style.

3. Glue or tape the head onto
   the body as shown.

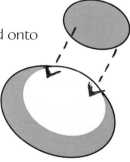

4. Attach the legs to the back of the body.
   Stick on the googly eyes. Draw a smile.

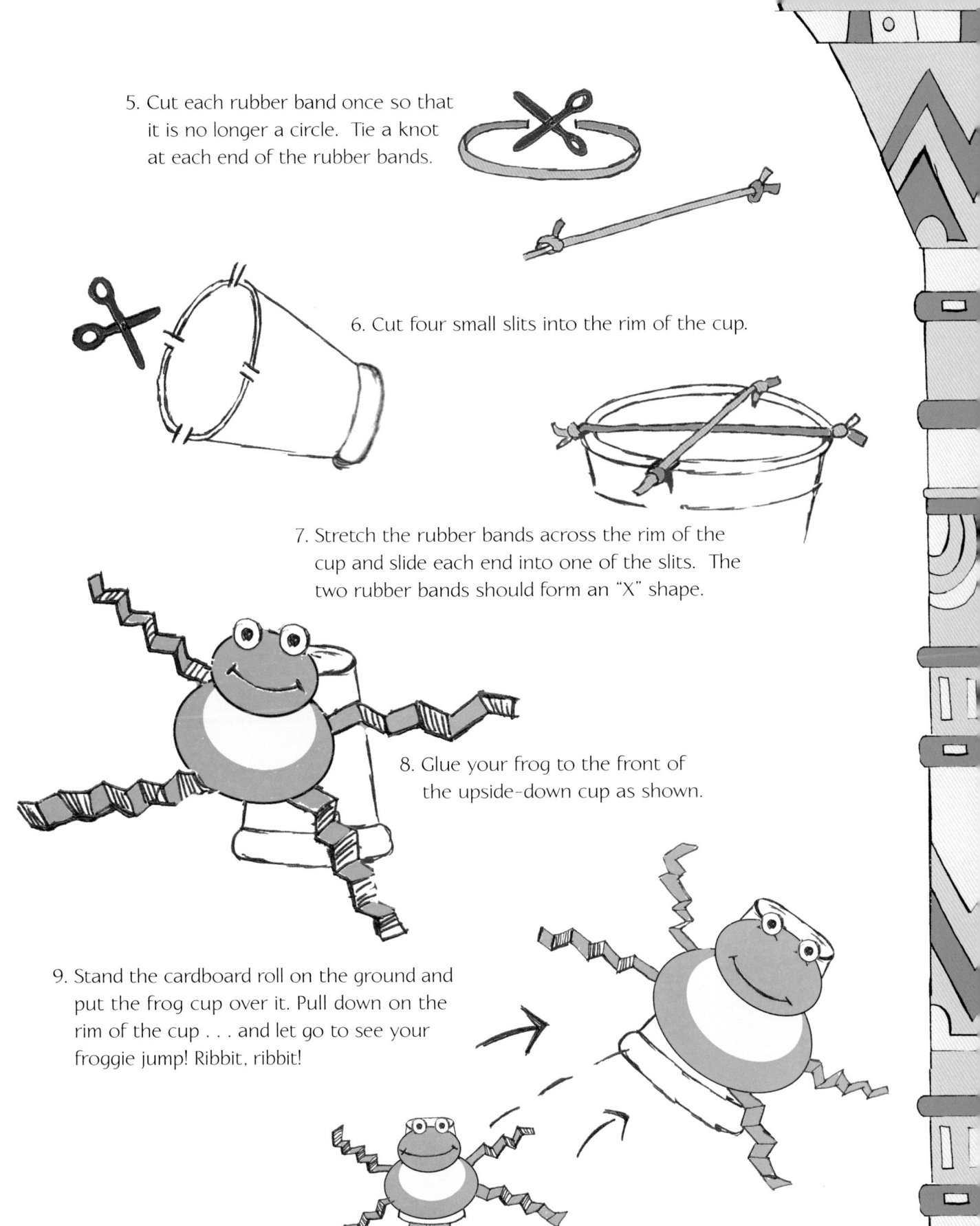

5. Cut each rubber band once so that it is no longer a circle. Tie a knot at each end of the rubber bands.

6. Cut four small slits into the rim of the cup.

7. Stretch the rubber bands across the rim of the cup and slide each end into one of the slits. The two rubber bands should form an "X" shape.

8. Glue your frog to the front of the upside-down cup as shown.

9. Stand the cardboard roll on the ground and put the frog cup over it. Pull down on the rim of the cup . . . and let go to see your froggie jump! Ribbit, ribbit!

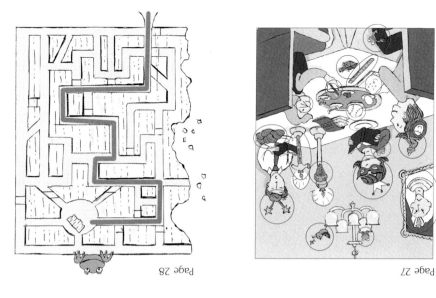

Page 27

Page 28

Answers

Page 18: (clockwise from top) beitzah=rebirth, zeroa=lamb, charoset=mortar, maror=bitterness, chazeret=bitterness, karpas=spring

Page 19: the second cup is different (color of diamonds on the rim and dots on base)

One Morning (The Frog Song)

Shirley Cohen Steinberg

Voice

One morm - ing when Phar - aoh a - woke in bed, there were

Vo.

frogs in the bed and frogs on his head, frogs on his nose and

Vo.

frogs on his toes. Frogs here! Frogs there! Frogs just jump - ing ev - ery - where!